This igloo book belongs to:

....

Contents

The New Friend 4

Little Brother Blues 14

Mum to the Rescue 24

The Rainy Day 32

Sam's Sleepover.................... 42

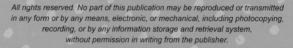

igloobooks

Published in 2017
by Igloo Books Ltd, Cottage Farm, Sywell, NN6 0BJ
www.igloobooks.com

Written by Annamaria Farbizio
Illustrated by Giulia Rivolta

Designed by Stephanie Drake
Edited by Stephanie Moss

STA002 1117
2 4 6 8 10 9 7 5 3 1
ISBN 978-1-78670-749-9

Printed and manufactured in China

Stories for 4 Year Olds

igloobooks

The New Friend

Helen sat glumly on the garden swing. She had
just moved to a new town with her mum and dad,
but she **really** missed her old friends.

It was no fun playing by herself, but she
felt too shy to make any new friends.

Suddenly, Helen felt something **bounce** off her head and onto the grass.

It was a big, purple ball.

Ouch, that hurt!

she cried.

Oh, sorry. My name's Brad. What's yours?

asked a voice, from over the fence.

Helen's head **throbbed** and she felt annoyed. But Brad sounded friendly, so she replied.

Helen said yes, so Brad **jumped** over the fence.

Hello, I'm Helen,

she said.

Hold on tight!

he said.

Would you like to play? I can push you on your swing,

said Brad.

Brad gave Helen a **huge** push and the swing went **really** high!

Woo-hoo!

cried Helen.

It wasn't long before Helen felt dizzy and she wanted to do something else.

Shall we play catch?

asked Brad.

Okay, you start,

said Helen.

Helen and Brad threw the ball...

... backwards and forwards...

... higher and higher.

Good catch!

called Brad.

When it was time for a new game, it was Helen's turn to come up with an idea. She thought hard until she had the perfect plan.

Let's build a den,

said Helen.

So they tied some branches together and draped a blanket over them, then put some cushions and blankets inside. Soon, the den was finished and it looked **amazing.**

9

Brad and Helen pretended they were explorers, **creeping** quietly through the jungle.

Then, they ran back to their den, **giggling** and **laughing.**

Later on, Mum and Dad came outside to say hello.

This is my new friend, Brad,

said Helen.

So, Mum brought them some sandwiches and orange juice as a **special** treat.

Then, Dad fetched the paddling pool and filled it with water.

Wow, thank you!

cried Helen.

They tucked into the tasty snacks, before setting off to play more games.

Next, Brad and Helen played pirate dress-up together. Helen **squealed** with delight when Brad pretended to be a sea monster.

Mum and Dad laughed. They were so happy to see that Helen had cheered up and was having **so much** fun.

When it was time to go, Brad said
thank you and waved goodbye.

See you tomorrow,

he said.

We'll think of even more games to play!

said Helen.

She waved and smiled.
Helen was going to **love**
her new home!

Little Brother Blues

Sally was **fed up** of her little brother, Robbie. He always wanted to play with all of her best toys and he was always making a mess. Mum said that Robbie was only little, but Sally didn't care!

One morning, Sally had neatly arranged everything in her doll's house, when Robbie **burst** into her room.

I want to play with the toys!

he cried.

No, don't!

cried Sally.

But it was too late. Robbie had knocked everything over.

15

Sally felt **really** annoyed.
Robbie was spoiling her whole playtime.

I wish he would just play by himself,

she thought, pulling a grumpy face.

Robbie just giggled, which made Sally feel even more annoyed.

Next, Sally got out her paints to play with, but Robbie got really excited as well.

I want to play, too!

he cried.

Robbie **giggled** and plopped a brush in the pots. Paint **splattered** everywhere.

Oh, Robbie, look what you've done!

cried Sally.

17

Sally felt so annoyed, she picked up her teddy and went downstairs.

Sally, wait for me!

called Robbie.

No, I'm going outside to play,

she said.

Sally put her teddy in a little red wagon.

You can go for a ride with the other toys,

she said.

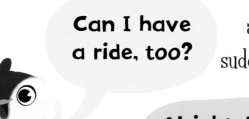

Can I have a ride, too? asked Robbie, suddenly appearing.

Alright, but be careful, or you'll tip it over,

replied Sally.

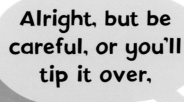

Robbie went to step into the wagon, but just like Sally had said, he made it topple over!

The toys all went **flying** out of the wagon.

She ran upstairs and stuck a sign to her bedroom door so that Robbie couldn't come in. Sally played happily with her dolls and Robbie wasn't around to spoil anything. It was perfect!

When Sally had arranged all her doll's house furniture, she painted a picture. Then, she didn't know what to do!

She was so used to Robbie being around, Sally suddenly realised that she actually missed him.

Sally thought long and hard to come up with a game she and Robbie could play happily together. Then, she had an idea.

Shall we play hide-and-seek?

she asked.

Yes, please!

cried Robbie.

So, Sally counted to 10 and Robbie went to hide, but he wasn't very difficult to find!

Boo, found you!

cried Sally.

Robbie **squealed** with laughter.

They played games all afternoon and Sally realised she was having lots of fun. Maybe having a little brother wasn't so bad after all.

23

Mum to the Rescue

It was the day before Grandma's birthday and Katie had lots of lovely things planned for her. She was so excited to get started, that Katie **tumbled** right out of bed and onto the floor.

Let me help you up,

said Mum, **rushing** into Katie's bedroom.

After breakfast, Katie got dressed. She was in such a hurry to pull on her best jumper, that she tore a **great big** hole in it.

Later that morning, Katie had just started to make a special birthday card for Grandma, when she knocked **sparkly** rainbow glitter all over the table.

I'd better clean that up,

said Mum, getting a wet cloth straight away.

Mum was there to help when Katie tried to knit Grandma a scarf.

She quickly turned off the hose when Katie picked Grandma flowers.

Mum even helped Katie pick up all the beads for Grandma's necklace. 27

So, Mum invited Katie's friend, Molly, round to come and play and said she would help to get everything ready for Grandma's birthday, instead.

They had a **fantastic** time, playing in the garden all afternoon. Then, Katie wanted to take turns riding on her new bike.

So, Katie climbed on first, but then, Molly pointed to one of the bike wheels.

It's flat!

she said.

I'll fix it!

said Mum.

Sure enough, she was there with a toolbox, ready to help!

When Molly went home, Katie looked everywhere for Mum. She found her making a cake in the kitchen, **completely** covered in flour.

It's my turn to help, now!

said Katie, grabbing an apron.

It looks really yummy,

said Katie, adding a candle to the top of the cake.

It does. Thanks for coming to my rescue,

said Mum.

The Rainy Day

One day, Josh came to Amanda's house to play. They had planned lots of fun games in the garden and Josh couldn't wait to start.

Hurry up, Amanda!

he called.

Coming!

she cried.

Amanda **bounded** down the garden path, ready to play. Then, just as he was about to throw the ball, Josh thought he felt a drop of rain.

Josh felt two more drops...

...then three...

...then four.

**Oh, no...
it's raining!**

he cried.

Lightning **flashed** across the sky and
thunder **rumbled**. Josh and Amanda **dashed** back inside.

Amanda and Josh watched the raindrops **splatter** on the window from inside. They felt **so** disappointed. Playing inside was boring.

Cheer up. You could play hide-and-seek, instead?

suggested Mum,

I suppose so,

said Amanda, sadly.

First, it was Josh's turn
to count to 10.

Amanda hid behind a plant.

She tried hard
not to giggle.

Boo,
found you!

cried Josh.

**Let's see
what's in the
attic, next,**

said Amanda,
pointing upstairs.

Amanda's mum unlocked the attic and let Josh and Amanda explore.
They found an old rocking horse, a dusty doll's house and some toy cars.

Then, Amanda found a wooden box, full of dressing-up clothes.
She **gasped** and put on a sparkly dress and a tiara.

I'm a princess!

cried Amanda.

Then, Josh found a magician's
costume and a magic wand.

I'm a real
magician!

he cried.

Princess Amanda and Josh the Magician ran downstairs to play.

Abracadabra!
Rain disappear, away from here!

cried Josh.

He waved his wand at the window, and, as if by magic...

... the rain stopped and a sunbeam shone into the room!

Wow, you really are a magician!

cried Amanda.

Let's go outside and play!

cried Josh.

Amanda's mum gave them some rubber boots to wear and they ran into the garden at last.

Outside, the rain on the grass was **sparkling** with sunshine and there was a beautiful rainbow in the sky.

It's just like a magical fairy garden. I wish we had a fairy feast,

said Amanda.

Suddenly, Amanda's mum appeared with some
sandwiches and drinks. Josh and Amanda giggled.
This was the best playtime ever!

41

Sam's Sleepover

Sam was the smallest of all his friends, but he knew he could be just as **big** and **brave** as them. So, he invited Tilly and Dan round for a super-spooky sleepover. When they got there, he turned off the lights and grabbed his torch.

They followed Sam upstairs, when suddenly, they saw a **spooky** shadow on the wall.

They both felt scared, until they saw Sam making shapes with his toy dino in the dark!

When they'd all snuggled up in their sleeping bags, there were **creepy** noises echoing all around Sam's room.

BANG!

BANG!

BANG!

What's that noise?

asked Dan.

Dan and Tilly looked around for the strange sound, but it was only Sam, **banging** his toy drum.

44

Soon, it was time for a midnight feast. Sam was feeling so brave, he couldn't help telling a spooky story on the way downstairs.

A monster lives in our kitchen,

he whispered.

Sam told Dan and Tilly that the monster was called the Cookie Gobbler...

... and that he only came out at night.

Slowly, Sam opened the kitchen door and peeked inside, sure his friends would be scared. Instead, he saw a dark shadow that looked just like the monster he'd told them about!

Sam peered in closer and switched on the kitchen light. Then, he breathed a sigh of relief. It was only Dad, **munching** on cookies! Tilly and Dan both laughed.

You weren't the only ones who fancied a midnight snack!

chuckled Dad.

Sam, Dan and Tilly went back upstairs and switched all the lights back on. They spent the rest of the night **snuggled** together, drinking hot chocolate and telling each other not-so-spooky stories!